Turbo Turtle
to the Rescue

by Jeff Dinardo • illustrated by Jim Paillot

RED
CHAIR
•PRESS•

It was late at night.
Turbo Turtle settled into his cozy chair.
He had a glass of milk and his favorite book.

"Finally time to relax," he said.
Just then the Turtle Phone started to ring.
RING RING, RING RING.

Turbo Turtle jumped up.
He put the Turtle Phone to his ear.
"Hi Chief," he said. "What's wrong?"

4

"We need you," said the Chief.
"Duck Girl is causing problems!"
"I'm on my way!" Turbo Turtle said.

Turbo Turtle flew over the city.
He used his turtle vision and
saw the trouble.

Duck Girl was trying to rob the bunny troop. "Give me all your ice cream!" she demanded.

"Not so fast!" said Turbo Turtle
as he swooped in.
"I am here to stop you."

The bunny troop cheered.
"Not if I stop you first!" said Duck Girl.
She took out her zapping ray.

ZAP

Pink slime shot out just missing Turbo Turtle.
He jumped out of the way.
"Bubble gum!" he said.

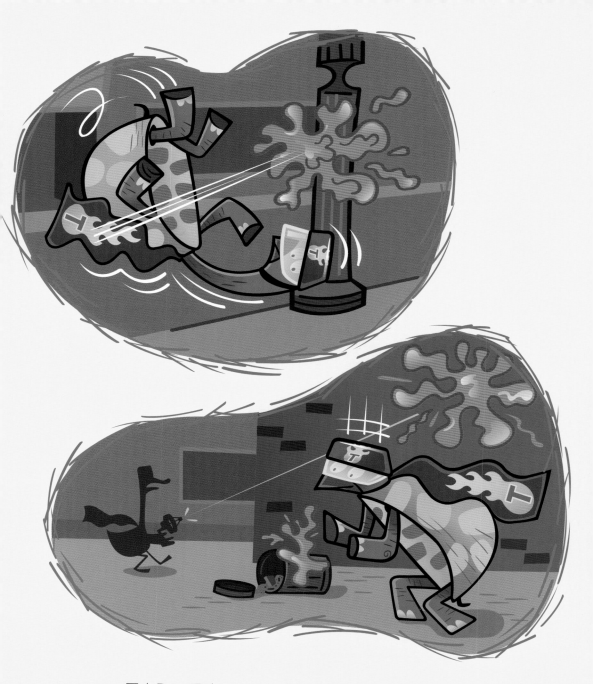

ZAP, ZAP, ZAP
The bubble gum kept flying.
Turbo Turtle narrowly escaped.

Turbo Turtle grabbed some gum.
He put it into his mouth and chewed.
He blew a huge bubble right at Duck Girl.

SPLAT
It popped, trapping her in her own gum.

The Chief took Duck Girl to jail.
The bunny troop thanked Turbo Turtle.
They even gave him some ice cream.

Then Turbo Turtle flew home.
He got back into his favorite chair
and finally read his book.

Big Question: How did the bunny troop show Turbo Turtle they were grateful for his help?

Big Words:

escaped: got away from danger

settled: got comfortable

swooped: moved down fast

vision: the ability to see